Travel and Transport
Then and Now

Written by Alastair Smith

Designed by Ruth Russell

Illustrated by Adrienne Salgado

Series editor: Judy Tatchell

Early days

Long, long ago, travel was slow. People had to walk if they wanted to get from place to place.

We're off to find our dinner.

For water travel, they learned how to make simple boats.

Hollowed-out log

Four legs are faster than two.

Later on, people rode animals to help them get around.

This is how they might have carried heavy things.

Whew!

Nobody had cars, planes or bikes. They hadn't been invented.

Great ideas

Over the years, some clever inventions led to lots of new types of transport.

Wheels let things move smoothly over the ground.

Early wheelbarrow

Engines gave vehicles power to move quickly.

Early car

Wings allowed planes to soar high into the sky.

Early plane

These things helped people to travel more quickly and easily.

Long, long ago, it could take days to get from place to place.

My feet are sore.

On the water

Before boats were invented, people sat on logs when they wanted to cross water. The logs floated, but they were wobbly.

Less wobbly

Then people tried making rafts by tying logs together. These were less wobbly.

I use this piece of wood as a paddle.

Boats to carry things

Boats could hold more if they were hollow in the middle.

Animal skin stretched over a wooden frame

I can get lots of fish in here.

Wind power

To move more quickly, people used the wind. They put sails on their boats. The more sails they used, the more wind they could catch.

This type of boat was built about 150 years ago.

Here's a picture of one of the very first sailing boats. It was built about 4,000 years ago. It only had one sail.

I'm steering.

When the wind was blowing, the boat moved easily.

On, over and through

The first roads were just tracks worn into the ground. In dry weather they were dusty and hard. In wet weather they became really boggy.

Dusty track

Roman roads

About 2,000 years ago, the Romans came up with a way to build hard, smooth roads. Their roads didn't get too dusty or boggy.

Roman road

Building a road

Romans built their roads in layers. Modern roads are built in layers, too.

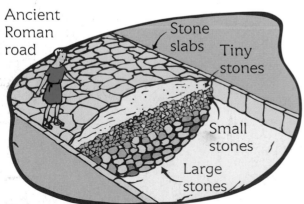

Ancient Roman road

Stone slabs

Tiny stones

Small stones

Large stones

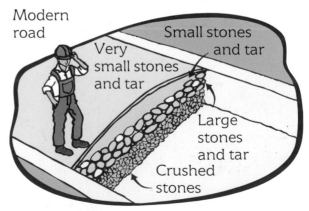

Modern road

Small stones and tar

Very small stones and tar

Large stones and tar

Crushed stones

Building bridges

Before bridges were invented, people had to go through rivers and streams to get to the other side.

Bridges made crossings a lot quicker and easier.

Too steep

People used to have to go over or around big steep mountains.

This took ages and was hard work.

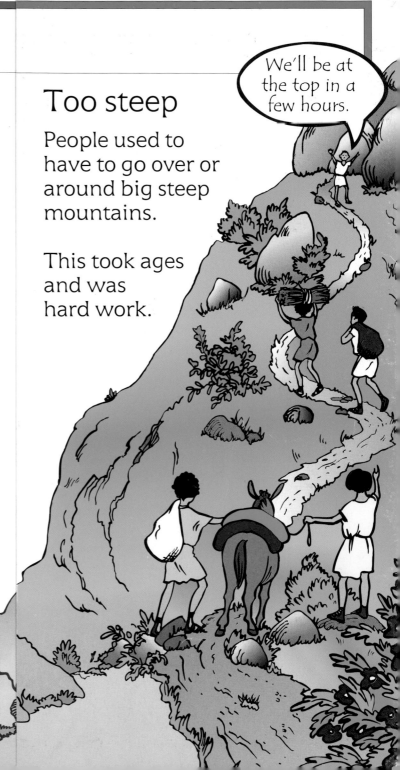

Take the train

The first trains were slow and noisy. The engines burned coal, which gave off lots of dirty smoke. Many passengers had to sit in the open air.

This is really hot work!

Oh no! It's raining.

It took a lot of fuel to keep a big train going. A man had to keep putting coal into the engine.

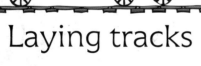

Laying tracks

Tracks were built all over the world for trains to run on. Laying tracks was hard work. But then lots of trains could use them.

First, workers made the land as flat as possible.

Then they laid the heavy metal tracks on top of wooden blocks.

Travel in style

In trains, people could travel more quickly than ever before. Some trains were very comfortable, but it cost a lot of money to travel on them.

Long journeys

On some long journeys, people were on the train for days. Passengers had their own rooms, called berths.

Bikes

The very first type of bike didn't have brakes, pedals or tyres. It wasn't comfortable at all.

He pushes with his feet to make the bike go.

This type of bike was called a hobbyhorse.

This bike had pedals. The rider used them to turn the front wheel. The wheels were made of metal. They made the ride very bumpy.

Judder judder

This type of bike was called a boneshaker.

Bouncy bikes

Inventors tried to make bikes more comfortable to ride. Here are some of their ideas.

Bouncy, air-filled tyres

Bouncy seat

Bouncy front wheel

A bike for two

This type of bike was invented for two people to ride at the same time. It's called a tandem.

Two can go faster than one.

On three wheels

Bikes with three wheels are called tricycles. Two people could sit on this one.

I do the steering.

Going faster

Bikes like this were so fast that people raced on them.

The back wheel is tiny.

The huge front wheel covered lots of ground each time it went around. This is why the bike could go so fast.

Cars

The first cars were made from horse carriages. Instead of horses, they had engines to make them go.

These cars were slow and noisy. Many horses and people were scared of them.

Chug! Bang!

This car has its engine at the back.

For the rich

At first, only rich people could afford cars. Later on, car makers found ways to build cars more cheaply and quickly.

More people could afford to buy the cheaper cars.

Expensive car

This is a Rolls-Royce.

Hundreds of these Ford Model Ts could be put together in a factory every day.

Cheaper car

Shapes and sizes

Since the early days, car makers have come up with all sorts of different cars.

Some are built for speed, like this Lamborghini.

Some cars are amazing to look at, like this Jaguar.

Some carry more people, like this people carrier.

Smaller cars

Today, there are lots and lots of cars. The roads are very crowded. Many people choose to drive small, nippy cars.

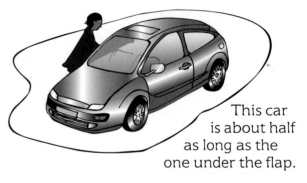

This car is about half as long as the one under the flap.

Lift the flap to see the rest of this pink monster.

Cars were bigger before the roads got so crowded.

Up in the air

For thousands of years people have wanted to fly. But for a long, long time nobody could figure out how to do it. Flying was a mystery.

How do they do that?

I don't know.

First attempts

Some people tried to fly by attaching wings to their arms. This never worked.

Success at last

People realized that the wing shape had to be just right. About 100 years ago, inventors figured it out. Soon they built the first planes.

Aaargh!

His wings are the wrong shape. And he's too heavy!

His arms aren't strong enough.

The wings wouldn't work unless they were curved like this.

Plane power

At first, all planes had propellers. These spun around to pull the plane through the air.

Engines made the propellers spin.

About 60 years ago jet engines were invented. They blast air backwards to push a plane forwards.

Jet planes are faster than propeller planes.

No wings

You can travel through the air without wings or an engine. You would need lots of hot air, though.

Open the flap and you'll see lift off.

Index

With thanks to Dr. Anne Millard.

First published in 2000 by Usborne Publishing Ltd, 83-85 Saffron Hill, London EC1N 8RT, England.
www.usborne.com

Printed in Hong Kong, China.

ROALD DAHL

REVOLTING
Rhymes

ILLUSTRATED BY QUENTIN BLAKE

PUFFIN

Find out more about Roald Dahl
by visiting the website at
roalddahl.com

PUFFIN BOOKS

Published by the Penguin Group
Penguin Books Ltd, 80 Strand, London WC2R 0RL, England
Penguin Group (USA) Inc., 375 Hudson Street, New York, New York 10014, USA
Penguin Group (Canada), 90 Eglinton Avenue East, Suite 700, Toronto, Ontario, Canada M4P 2Y3
(a division of Pearson Penguin Canada Inc.)
Penguin Ireland, 25 St Stephen's Green, Dublin 2, Ireland (a division of Penguin Books Ltd)
Penguin Group (Australia), 707 Collins Street, Melbourne, Victoria 3008, Australia
(a division of Pearson Australia Group Pty Ltd)
Penguin Books India Pvt Ltd, 11 Community Centre, Panchsheel Park, New Delhi – 110 017, India
Penguin Group (NZ), 67 Apollo Drive, Rosedale, North Shore 0632, New Zealand
(a division of Pearson New Zealand Ltd)
Penguin Books (South Africa) (Pty) Ltd, Block D, Rosebank Office Park, 181 Jan Smuts Avenue,
Parktown North, Gauteng 2193, South Africa

Penguin Books Ltd, Registered Offices: 80 Strand, London WC2R 0RL, England

puffinbooks.com

First published by Jonathan Cape Ltd 1982
Published by Puffin Books 1984
This edition published 2013
001

Text copyright © Roald Dahl Nominee Ltd, 1982
Illustrations copyright © Quentin Blake, 1982, 1984, 2001
All rights reserved

The moral right of the author and illustrator has been asserted

Made and printed in China

British Library Cataloguing in Publication Data
A CIP catalogue record for this book is available from the British Library

ISBN: 978–0–141–35037–0

ALWAYS LEARNING   **PEARSON**

CONTENTS

Cinderella

I guess you think you know this story.
  You don't. The real one's much more gory.
The phoney one, the one you know,
Was cooked up years and years ago,
And made to sound all soft and sappy
Just to keep the children happy.
Mind you, they got the first bit right,
The bit where, in the dead of night,
The Ugly Sisters, jewels and all,
Departed for the Palace Ball,
While darling little Cinderella
Was locked up in a slimy cellar,
Where rats who wanted things to eat,
Began to nibble at her feet.

She bellowed 'Help!' and 'Let me out!'
The Magic Fairy heard her shout.
Appearing in a blaze of light,
She said, 'My dear, are you all right?'
'*All right?*' cried Cindy. 'Can't you see
'I feel as rotten as can be!'
She beat her fist against the wall,
And shouted, 'Get me to the Ball!
'There is a Disco at the Palace!
'The rest have gone and I am jalous!
'I want a dress! I want a coach!
'And earrings and a diamond brooch!
'And silver slippers, two of those!
'And lovely nylon panty-hose!
'Done up like that I'll guarantee
'The handsome Prince will fall for me!'
The Fairy said, 'Hang on a tick.'
She gave her wand a mighty flick
And quickly, in no time at all,
Cindy was at the Palace Ball!
It made the Ugly Sisters wince
To see her dancing with the Prince.
She held him very tight and pressed
Herself against his manly chest.
The Prince himself was turned to pulp,
All *he* could do was gasp and gulp.

Then midnight struck. She shouted, 'Heck!
'I've got to run to save my neck!'
The Prince cried, 'No! Alas! Alack!'
He grabbed her dress to hold her back.
As Cindy shouted, 'Let me go!'
The dress was ripped from head to toe.
She ran out in her underwear,
And lost one slipper on the stair.
The Prince was on it like a dart,
He pressed it to his pounding heart,
'The girl this slipper fits,' he cried,
'Tomorrow morn shall be my bride!
'I'll visit every house in town
'Until I've tracked the maiden down!'
Then rather carelessly, I fear,
He placed it on a crate of beer.
At once, one of the Ugly Sisters,
(The one whose face was blotched with blisters)
Sneaked up and grabbed the dainty shoe,
And quickly flushed it down the loo.

Then in its place she calmly put
The slipper from her own left foot.
Ah-ha, you see, the plot grows thicker,
And Cindy's luck starts looking sicker.
Next day, the Prince went charging down
To knock on all the doors in town.
In every house, the tension grew.
Who was the owner of the shoe?
The shoe was long and very wide.
(A normal foot got lost inside.)
Also it smelled a wee bit icky.
(The owner's feet were hot and sticky.)
Thousands of eager people came
To try it on, but all in vain.
Now came the Ugly Sisters' go.
One tried it on. The Prince screamed, 'No!'
But she screamed, 'Yes! It fits! Whoopee!
'So now you've got to marry me!'
The Prince went white from ear to ear.
He muttered, 'Let me out of here.'
'Oh no you don't! You made a vow!

'There's no way you can back out now!'
'Off with her head!' the Prince roared back.
They chopped it off with one big whack.
This pleased the Prince. He smiled and said,
'She's prettier without her head.'
Then up came Sister Number Two,
Who yelled, 'Now *I* will try the shoe!'
'Try this instead!' the Prince yelled back.
He swung his trusty sword and *smack* –
Her head went crashing to the ground.
It bounced a bit and rolled around.
In the kitchen, peeling spuds,
Cinderella heard the thuds
Of bouncing heads upon the floor,
And poked her own head round the door.
'What's all the racket?' Cindy cried.
'Mind your own bizz,' the Prince replied.
Poor Cindy's heart was torn to shreds.
My Prince! She thought. He chops off *heads*!

How could I marry anyone
Who does that sort of thing for fun?
The Prince cried, 'Who's this dirty slut?
'Off with her nut! Off with her nut!'
Just then, all in a blaze of light,
The Magic Fairy hove in sight,
Her Magic Wand went *swoosh* and *swish*!
'Cindy!' she cried, 'come make a wish!
'Wish anything and have no doubt
'That I will make it come about!'
Cindy answered, 'Oh kind Fairy,
'This time I shall be more wary.
'No more Princes, no more money.
'I have had my taste of honey.
'I'm wishing for a decent man.
'They're hard to find. D'you think you can?'
Within a minute, Cinderella
Was married to a lovely feller,
A simple jam-maker by trade,
Who sold good home-made marmalade.
Their house was filled with smiles and laughter
And they were happy ever after.

Jack and the Beanstalk

Jack's mother said, 'We're *stony broke*!
  'Go out and find some wealthy bloke
'Who'll buy our cow. Just say she's sound
'And worth at least a hundred pound.
'But don't you dare to let him know
'That she's as old as billy-o.'
Jack led the old brown cow away,
And came back later in the day,
And said, 'Oh mumsie dear, guess what
'Your clever little boy has got.
'I got, I really don't know how,
'A super trade-in for our cow.'
The mother said, 'You little creep,
'I'll bet you sold her much too cheap.'

When Jack produced one lousy bean,
His startled mother, turning green,
Leaped high up in the air and cried,
'I'm *absolutely stupefied*!
'You crazy boy! D'you really mean
'You sold our Daisy for a bean?'
She snatched the bean. She yelled, 'You chump!'
And flung it on the rubbish-dump.
Then summoning up all her power,
She beat the boy for half an hour,
Using (and nothing could be meaner)
The handle of a vacuum-cleaner.
At ten p.m. or thereabout,
The little bean began to sprout.
By morning it had grown so tall
You couldn't see the top at all.
Young Jack cried, 'Mum, admit it now!
'It's better than a rotten cow!'
The mother said, 'You lunatic!
'Where are the beans that I can pick?
'There's not *one bean*! It's bare as bare!'
'No no!' cried Jack. 'You look up there!
'Look very high and you'll behold
'Each single leaf is solid gold!'
By gollikins, the boy was right!
Now, glistening in the morning light,
The mother actually perceives
A mass of lovely golden leaves!

She yells out loud, 'My sainted souls!
'I'll sell the Mini, buy a Rolls!
'Don't stand and gape, you little clot!
'Get up there quick and grab the lot!'
Jack was nimble, Jack was keen.
He scrambled up the mighty bean.
Up up he went without a stop,
But just as he was near the top,
A ghastly frightening thing occurred –
Not far above his head he heard
A big deep voice, a rumbling thing
That made the very heavens ring.
It shouted loud, 'FEE FI FO FUM
'I SMELL THE BLOOD OF AN
    ENGLISHMAN!'
Jack was frightened, Jack was quick,
And down he climbed in half a tick.

16

'Oh mum!' he gasped. 'Believe you me
'There's something nasty up our tree!
'I saw him, mum! My gizzard froze!
'A Giant with a clever nose!'
'*A clever nose*!' his mother hissed.
'You must be going round the twist!'
'He smelled me out, I swear it, mum!
'He said he *smelled* an Englishman!'
The mother said, 'And well he might!
'I've told you every single night
'To take a bath because you smell,
'But would you do it? Would you hell!
'You even make your mother shrink
'Because of your unholy stink!'
Jack answered, 'Well, if you're so clean
'Why don't *you* climb the crazy bean.'

The mother cried, 'By gad, I will!
'There's life within the old dog still!'
She hitched her skirts above her knee
And disappeared right up the tree.
Now would the Giant smell his mum?
Jack listened for the *fee-fo-fum*.
He gazed aloft. He wondered when
The dreaded words would come . . . And then . . .
From somewhere high above the ground
There came a frightful crunching sound.
He heard the Giant mutter twice,
'By gosh, that tasted very nice.
'Although' (and this in grumpy tones)
'I wish there weren't so many bones.'
'By Christopher!' Jack cried. 'By gum!
'The Giant's eaten up my mum!
'He smelled her out! She's in his belly!
'I had a hunch that she was smelly.'
Jack stood there gazing longingly
Upon the huge and golden tree.
He murmured softly, 'Golly-gosh,
'I guess I'll *have* to take a wash
'If I am going to climb this tree
'Without the Giant smelling me.
'In fact, a bath's my only hope . . .'
He rushed indoors and grabbed the soap.
He scrubbed his body everywhere.
He even washed and rinsed his hair.

He did his teeth, he blew his nose
And went out smelling like a rose.
Once more he climbed the mighty bean.
The Giant sat there, gross, obscene,
Muttering through his vicious teeth
(While Jack sat tensely just beneath),
Muttering loud, 'FEE FI FO FUM,
'RIGHT NOW I CAN'T SMELL ANYONE.'
Jack waited till the Giant slept,
Then out along the boughs he crept
And gathered so much gold, I swear
He was an instant millionaire.
'A bath,' he said, 'does seem to pay.
'I'm going to have one every day.'

Snow-White and the Seven Dwarfs

When little Snow-White's mother died,
The king, her father, up and cried,
'Oh, what a nuisance! What a life!
'Now I must find another wife!'
(It's never easy for a king
To find himself that sort of thing.)
He wrote to every magazine
And said, 'I'm looking for a Queen.'
At least ten thousand girls replied
And begged to be the royal bride.
The king said with a shifty smile,
'I'd like to give each one a trial.'
However, in the end he chose
A lady called Miss Maclahose,
Who brought along a curious toy
That seemed to give her endless joy –
This was a mirror framed in brass,
A MAGIC TALKING LOOKING-GLASS.
Ask it something day or night,
It always got the answer right.
For instance, if you were to say,
'Oh Mirror, what's for lunch today?'
The thing would answer in a trice,

'Today it's scrambled eggs and rice.'
Now every day, week in week out,
The spoiled and stupid Queen would shout,
'Oh Mirror Mirror on the wall,
'Who is the fairest of them all?'
The Mirror answered every time,
'Oh Madam, you're the Queen sublime.
'You are the only one to charm us,
'Queen, you are the cat's pyjamas.'
For ten whole years the silly Queen
Repeated this absurd routine.
Then suddenly, one awful day,
She heard the Magic Mirror say,
'From now on, Queen, you're *Number Two*.
'*Snow-White* is prettier than you!'
The Queen went absolutely wild.
She yelled, 'I'm going to scrag that child!

'I'll cook her flaming goose! I'll skin 'er!
'I'll have her rotten guts for dinner!'
She called the Huntsman to her study.
She shouted at him, 'Listen, buddy!
'You drag that filthy girl outside,
'And see you take her for a ride!
'Thereafter slit her ribs apart
'And bring me back her bleeding heart!'
The Huntsman dragged the lovely child
Deep deep into the forest wild.

Fearing the worst, poor Snow-White spake.
She cried, 'Oh please give me a break!'
The knife was poised, the arm was strong,
She cried again, 'I've done no *wrong*!'
The Huntsman's heart began to flutter.
It melted like a pound of butter.
He murmured, 'Okay, beat it, kid,'
And you can bet your life she did.

Later, the Huntsman made a stop
Within the local butcher's shop,
And there he bought, for safety's sake,
A bullock's heart and one nice steak.

'Oh Majesty! Oh Queen!' he cried,
'That rotten little girl has died!
'And just to prove I didn't cheat,
'I've brought along these bits of meat.'
The Queen cried out, 'Bravissimo!
'I trust you killed her nice and slow.'
Then (this is the disgusting part)
The Queen sat down and ate the heart!
(I only hope she cooked it well.
Boiled heart can be as tough as hell.)
While all of this was going on,
Oh where, oh where had Snow-White gone?
She'd found it easy, being pretty,
To hitch a ride into the city,
And there she'd got a job, unpaid,
As general cook and parlour-maid
With seven funny little men,
Each one not more than three foot ten,
Ex horse-race jockeys, all of them.

These Seven Dwarfs, though awfully nice,
Were guilty of one shocking vice –
They squandered all of their resources
At the race-track backing horses.
(When they hadn't backed a winner,
None of them got any dinner.)
One evening, Snow-White said, 'Look here,
'I think I've got a great idea.
'Just leave it all to me, okay?
'And no more gambling till I say.'
That very night, at eventide,
Young Snow-White hitched another ride,
And then, when it was very late,
She slipped in through the Palace gate.
The King was in his counting house
Counting out his money,
The Queen was in the parlour
Eating bread and honey,
The footmen and the servants slept
So no one saw her as she crept
On tip-toe through the mighty hall
And grabbed THE MIRROR off the wall.
As soon as she had got it home,
She told the Senior Dwarf (or Gnome)
To ask it what he wished to know.
'Go on!' she shouted. 'Have a go!'
He said, 'Oh Mirror, please don't joke!
'Each one of us is stony broke!
'Which horse will win tomorrow's race,

'The Ascot Gold Cup Steeplechase?'
The Mirror whispered sweet and low,
'The horse's name is Mistletoe.'
The Dwarfs went absolutely daft,
They kissed young Snow-White fore and aft,
Then rushed away to raise some dough
With which to back old Mistletoe.
They pawned their watches, sold the car,
They borrowed money near and far,
(For much of it they had to thank
The manager of Barclays Bank.)
They went to Ascot and of course
For once they backed the winning horse.
Thereafter, every single day,
The Mirror made the bookies pay.
Each Dwarf and Snow-White got a share,
And each was soon a millionaire,
Which shows that gambling's not a sin
Provided that you always win.

Goldilocks and the Three Bears

This famous wicked little tale
Should never have been put on sale.
It is a mystery to me
Why loving parents cannot see
That this is actually a book
About a brazen little crook.
Had I the chance I wouldn't fail
To clap young Goldilocks in jail.
Now just imagine how *you'd* feel
If you had cooked a lovely meal,
Delicious porridge, steaming hot,
Fresh coffee in the coffee-pot,
With maybe toast and marmalade,
The table beautifully laid,
One place for you and one for dad,
Another for your little lad.
Then dad cries, 'Golly-gosh! Gee-whizz!
'Oh cripes! How hot this porridge is!

'Let's take a walk along the street
'Until it's cool enough to eat.'
He adds, 'An early morning stroll
'Is good for people on the whole.
'It makes your appetite improve
'It also helps your bowels to move.'
No proper wife would dare to question
Such a sensible suggestion,
Above all not at breakfast-time
When men are seldom at their prime.
No sooner are you down the road
Than Goldilocks, that little toad,
That nosey thieving little louse,
Comes sneaking in your empty house.
She looks around. She quickly notes
Three bowls brimful of porridge oats.
And while still standing on her feet,
She grabs a spoon and starts to eat.

I say again, how *would* you feel
If you had made this lovely meal
And some delinquent little tot
Broke in and gobbled up the lot?

But wait! That's not the worst of it!
Now comes the most distressing bit.
You are of course a houseproud wife,
And all your happy married life
You have collected lovely things
Like gilded cherubs wearing wings,
And furniture by Chippendale
Bought at some famous auction sale.
But your most special valued treasure,
The piece that gives you endless pleasure,
Is one small children's dining-chair,
Elizabethan, very rare.
It is in fact your joy and pride,
Passed down to you on grandma's side.
But Goldilocks, like many freaks,
Does not appreciate antiques.
She doesn't care, she doesn't mind,
And now she plonks her fat behind
Upon this dainty precious chair,
And crunch! It busts beyond repair.
A nice girl would at once exclaim,
'Oh dear! Oh heavens! What a shame!'

Not Goldie. She begins to swear.
She bellows, 'What a lousy chair!'
And uses *one* disgusting word
That luckily you've never heard.
(I dare not write it, even hint it.
Nobody would ever print it.)
You'd think by now this little skunk
Would have the sense to do a bunk.
But no. I very much regret
She hasn't nearly finished yet.
Deciding she would like a rest,
She says, 'Let's see which bed is best.'
Upstairs she goes and tries all three.
(Here comes the next catastrophe.)
Most educated people choose
To rid themselves of socks and shoes
Before they clamber into bed.
But Goldie didn't give a shred.
Her filthy shoes were thick with grime,
And mud and mush and slush and slime.
Worse still, upon the heel of one
Was something that a dog had done.
I say once more, what *would* you think
If all this horrid dirt and stink
Was smeared upon your eiderdown
By this revolting little clown?
(The famous story has no clues
To show the girl removed her shoes.)

Oh, what a tale of crime on crime!
Let's check it for a second time.

Crime One, the prosecution's case:
She breaks and enters someone's place.

Crime Two, the prosecutor notes:
She steals a bowl of porridge oats.

Crime Three: She breaks a precious chair
Belonging to the Baby Bear.

Crime Four: She smears each spotless sheet
With filthy messes from her feet.

A judge would say without a blink,
'Ten years hard labour in the clink!'
But in the book, as you will see,
The little beast gets off scot-free,
While tiny children near and far
Shout, 'Goody-good! Hooray! Hurrah!'
'Poor darling Goldilocks!' they say,
'Thank goodness that she got away!'
Myself, I think I'd rather send
Young Goldie to a sticky end.
'Oh daddy!' cried the Baby Bear,
'My porridge gone! It isn't fair!'
'Then go upstairs,' the Big Bear said,
'Your porridge is upon the bed.
'But as it's inside mademoiselle,
'You'll have to eat *her* up as well.'

Little Red Riding Hood
and the Wolf

As soon as Wolf began to feel
   That he would like a decent meal,
He went and knocked on Grandma's door.
When Grandma opened it, she saw
The sharp white teeth, the horrid grin,
And Wolfie said, 'May I come in?'
Poor Grandmamma was terrified,
'He's going to eat me up,' she cried.
And she was absolutely right.
He ate her up in one big bite.
But Grandmamma was small and tough,
And Wolfie wailed, 'That's not enough!
'I haven't yet begun to feel
'That I have had a decent meal!'
He ran around the kitchen yelping,
'I've *got* to have another helping!'
Then added with a frightful leer,
'I'm therefore going to wait right here
'Till Little Miss Red Riding Hood
'Comes home from walking in the wood.'
He quickly put on Grandma's clothes.
(Of course he hadn't eaten those.)

He dressed himself in coat and hat.
He put on shoes and after that
He even brushed and curled his hair,
Then sat himself in Grandma's chair.
In came the little girl in red.
She stopped. She stared. And then she said,

'What great big ears you have, Grandma.'
'All the better to hear you with,' the Wolf replied.
'What great big eyes you have, Grandma,'
    said Little Red Riding Hood.
'All the better to see you with,' the Wolf replied.

He sat there watching her and smiled.
He thought, I'm going to eat this child.
Compared with her old Grandmamma
She's going to taste like caviare.

Then Little Red Riding Hood said, *'But Grandma,*
what a lovely great big furry coat you have on.'

38

'That's wrong!' cried Wolf. 'Have you forgot
'To tell me what BIG TEETH I've got?
'Ah well, no matter what you say,
'I'm going to eat you anyway.'
The small girl smiles. One eyelid flickers.
She whips a pistol from her knickers.
She aims it at the creature's head
And *bang bang bang,* she shoots him dead.
A few weeks later, in the wood,
I came across Miss Riding Hood.
But what a change! No cloak of red,
No silly hood upon her head.
She said, 'Hello, and do please note
'My lovely furry WOLFSKIN COAT.'

The Three Little Pigs

The animal I really dig
    Above all others is the pig.
Pigs are noble. Pigs are clever,
Pigs are courteous. However,
Now and then, to break this rule,
One meets a pig who is a fool.
What, for example, would you say
If strolling through the woods one day,
Right there in front of you you saw
A pig who'd built his house of STRAW?
The Wolf who saw it licked his lips,
And said, 'That pig has had his chips.'

'Little pig, little pig, let me come in!'
'No, no, by the hairs on my chinny-chin-chin!'
'Then I'll huff and I'll puff and I'll blow your
house in!'

The little pig began to pray,
But Wolfie blew his house away.
He shouted, 'Bacon, pork and ham!
'Oh, what a lucky Wolf I am!'
And though he ate the pig quite fast,
He carefully kept the tail till last.
Wolf wandered on, a trifle bloated.
Surprise, surprise, for soon he noted
Another little house for pigs,
And this one had been built of TWIGS!

'Little pig, little pig, let me come in!'
'No, no, by the hairs of my chinny-chin-chin!'
'Then I'll huff and I'll puff and I'll blow your
house in!'

The Wolf said 'Okay, here we go!'
He then began to blow and blow.
The little pig began to squeal.
He cried, 'Oh Wolf, you've had *one* meal!
'Why can't we talk and make a deal?'
The Wolf replied, 'Not on your nelly!'
And soon the pig was in his belly.
'Two juicy little pigs!' Wolf cried,
'But still I am not satisfied!
'I know full well my tummy's bulging,
'But oh, how I adore indulging.'

So creeping quietly as a mouse,
The Wolf approached another house,
A house which also had inside
A little piggy trying to hide.
But this one, Piggy Number Three,
Was bright and brainy as could be.
No straw for him, no twigs or sticks.
This pig had built his house of BRICKS.
'You'll not get *me*!' the Piggy cried.
'I'll blow you down!' the Wolf replied.
'You'll need,' Pig said, 'a lot of puff,
'And I don't think you've got enough.'
Wolf huffed and puffed and blew and blew.
The house stayed up as good as new.
'If I can't blow it *down*,' Wolf said,
'I'll have to blow it *up* instead.
'I'll come back in the dead of night
'And blow it up with dynamite!'
Pig cried, 'You brute! I might have known!'
Then, picking up the telephone,
He dialled as quickly as he could
The number of Red Riding Hood.

'Hello,' she said. 'Who's speaking? *Who?*

'Oh, hello Piggy, how d'you do?'

Pig cried, 'I need your help, Miss Hood!

'Oh help me, please! D'you think you could?'

'I'll try, of course,' Miss Hood replied.

'What's on your mind?' . . . '*A Wolf!*' Pig cried.

'I know you've dealt with wolves before,

'And now I've got one at my door!'

'My darling Pig,' she said, 'my sweet,

'That's something *really* up my street.

'I've just begun to wash my hair.

'But when it's dry, I'll be right there.'

A short while later, through the wood,

Came striding brave Miss Riding Hood.

The Wolf stood there, his eyes ablaze

And yellowish, like mayonnaise.

His teeth were sharp, his gums were raw,

And spit was dripping from his jaw.

Once more the maiden's eyelid flickers.
She draws the pistol from her knickers.
Once more, she hits the vital spot,
And kills him with a single shot.
Pig, peeping through the window, stood
And yelled, 'Well done, Miss Riding Hood!'

Ah, Piglet, you must never trust
Young ladies from the upper crust.
For now, Miss Riding Hood, one notes,
Not only has *two* wolfskin coats,
But when she goes from place to place,
She has a PIGSKIN TRAVELLING CASE.